Pete the Cat

Crayons Rock!

Matthew 6:34
—J.D.

To B.S.
Thank you for encouraging me every day!
Love always
—K.D.

ISBN 978-1-339-03199-6

12 11 10 9 8 7 6 5 4 3 2 1   23 24 25 26 27 28

Printed in the U.S.A.   40

First Scholastic printing, September 2023

The artist used pen and ink with watercolor and acrylic paint on 300lb press paper to create the illustrations for this book.

Kimberly & James Dean

Pete the Cat
Crayons Rock!

ROCKIN' RED

COOL CAT BLUE

SCHOLASTIC INC.

KEY WEST

Pete loves his big box of groovy crayons!
He loves to draw things like cars, trucks,
flowers, and trees.
    And most of all . . . the big blue sea.

From rockin' red
to cool cat blue,
with a box of crayons,
there's nothing
Pete can't do!

One day Pete decided to draw something new . . .

Using lots of colors is so much fun.
Pete wanted to use every one.
   He scribbled and drew a great big
smile. His drawings were groovy
and rockin' with style!

Pete was proud of the pictures he drew.
He hoped his friends would dig them, too.

Pete showed Grumpy Toad first.

Grumpy Toad said, "This doesn't look right. Those colors are way too bright."

Pete thought,

"HEY, NO SWEAT. THAT'S ALL RIGHT!"

Pete showed Gus his picture, too.

Gus asked, "Who is this supposed to be? It doesn't really look like me."

Pete thought,

"HEY, NO SWEAT. THAT'S ALL RIGHT!"

Pete finally showed Callie her picture.

Callie said, "This one is fine, but it feels like something's missing from mine."

Pete said,

"WHAT A

MESS!"

"Bummer. I guess my drawings aren't the best."
Pete started to frown. He put his crayons down.

In art class the teacher asked, "Pete what are you going to make?"
"I don't know—I'm afraid of making a mistake!"

Pete looked around.

Gus drew the coooooolest superheroes.

Callie's flowers were awesome! Out-of-sight!

Grumpy's motorcycle was just right!

Pete's heart sank. His paper was blank.

The gang looked at Pete and said,
"No sweat! It's all right!
"It doesn't have to be just right.

"Your art is cool because it's YOU.
Your art is so unique.

"Grab your groovy box of crayons.
Show us your technique!"

The teacher agreed. "Art should be fun!
Art is for everyone!

"From rockin' red
to cool cat blue,
with a box of crayons,
there's nothing you can't do!"

Pete smiled. "There are no rules. It's no big deal! Art is about how it makes you feel!"

Pete loved his cool art.
That's the one thing Pete knew.
Suddenly, Pete knew *exactly* what to do.

He tried again!

Instead of drawing them one by one,

Pete drew the whole gang, just having fun!

Grumpy Toad, Gus, and Callie agreed
Pete's picture was off the charts!
See? That's the groovy thing about art.

COOL
CAT
BLUE

MELLOW
YELLOW

CRAYONS

DEEP
PURPLE

ROCKIN
RED

CRAYONS

DEEP PURPLE

ORANGE TABBY

MELLOW YELLOW

COOL CAT BLUE

GROOVY GREEN

James Dean is the #1 *New York Times* bestselling creator and illustrator of Pete the Cat. He is a self-taught artist originally from Fort Payne, Alabama. He published his first book, *The Misadventures of Pete the Cat*, a history of his artwork, in 2006, and he illustrated his first children's book, *Pete the Cat: I Love My White Shoes*, in 2008. There are now dozens of published Pete the Cat titles, all inspired by James' real-life rescue pet.

Kimberly Dean is a children's author, artist, yoga enthusiast, and a #1 *New York Times* bestselling author. Before fulfilling her dream of becoming a full-time author and artist, she worked for the Governor's Press Office in the State of Georgia. Her dreams became a reality in 2013 with the release of her first children's book, *Pete the Cat and His Magic Sunglasses*. She has written many books since then, including *Willow and Oliver*. Kimberly lives in Savannah with her dog, Gypsy, and cat, Phoebe.